Milo's Big Mistake

Look out for other
LITTLE DOLPHIN titles:

Hattie's New House
Party Time, Poppy!
Oscar's Best Friends

Milo's Big Mistake

LUCY DANIELS

Illustrated by DAVID MELLING

AN
APPLE
PAPERBACK

Scholastic Inc.
New York   Toronto   London   Sydney
Mexico City   New Delhi   Hong Kong   Buenos Aires

ISBN 0-439-68198-7

Text copyright © 2004 by Working Partners Limited
Created by Working Partners Limited, London W6 0QT
Illustrations copyright © 2004 by David Melling

All rights reserved. Published by Scholastic Inc.,
557 Broadway, New York, NY 10012 by arrangement with
Working Partners Limited. LITTLE DOLPHIN is a trademark of
Working Partners Limited. SCHOLASTIC, APPLE PAPERBACKS,
and associated logos are trademarks and/or
registered trademarks of Scholastic Inc.

12 11 10 9 8 7 6 5 4   8 9 10/0

Printed in the U.S.A.
First Scholastic printing, February 2005

To a very special boy named Jamie Morgan
who likes all kinds of things, but especially stones,
stars, and dolphins. With much love.

Special thanks to Jan Burchett and Sara Vogler

CHAPTER ONE

"Look at me, Milo!" Little Dolphin called to his best friend. He flicked his tail and leaped out of the sea. "Bet you can't jump higher than that!" he whistled, as he plunged down below the surface again.

Little Dolphin and Milo were having a jumping competition in the middle of Urchin Bay.

They were leaping above the waves that rolled in from the ocean. Little Dolphin had only just learned how to jump, and now he wanted to do it all the time.

"Bet I *can* jump higher!" chirped Milo. "*And* I'll do a twist!"

He flipped his flippers and launched himself into the air. But suddenly, a big wave came from nowhere and knocked him into a spin!

He sank down through a school of mackerel, who scattered and darted away.

"What happened?" he
spluttered.

"A really big wave knocked
you over," Little Dolphin told him.

The two friends poked their
heads above the foamy waves.

"The sky's getting dark,"
clicked Milo. "Is it nighttime
already?"

"Of course not!" Little Dolphin grinned. "It isn't even afternoon yet. It's just clouds blocking out the sun."

They looked up at the dark clouds as they billowed across the sky.

"And the currents are really strong, too," Little Dolphin noticed. "I can feel them pulling me."

"Cool!" squeaked Milo.

"We've got all afternoon to play in them! Let's get started!"

"You're right," Little Dolphin agreed. "But there's one thing you've forgotten."

Milo looked puzzled. "Let me think," he said. "I'm here. You're here. The waves are here. So what is it?"

"You're such a scatterbrain, Milo!" Little Dolphin exclaimed. "You're coming to my cave for lunch!"

"Oh, I forgot!" chirped Milo. "I wondered why my tummy was making such funny noises!"

"Race you back home,"

Little Dolphin whistled. "And after lunch we'll get Poppy. She'll love these waves!"

They sped along the reef that grew in the middle of Urchin Bay, dived under a clump of pink coral, and darted inside Little Dolphin's cave.

"Slow down, you two!" clicked Little Dolphin's mom,

as she arranged lunch on the rock table. "You're making me dizzy!"

"Sorry, Mom," Little Dolphin chirped. "The waves are really high today!"

"And we want to play in them!" added Milo, gobbling down a big bite of food.

"Michael the weather fish has said there's a big storm coming," warned Little Dolphin's mom. "I'm going to store everything safely until it's gone."

"I've never seen a big storm before," Little Dolphin whistled. "What will happen?"

"There'll be heavy rain and strong winds," his mom told him as she put away her rare shell collection. "There might even be thunder and lightning," she warned. "And of course, the waves will be huge."

"Wow, I can't wait!" Little Dolphin squeaked.

The two friends were so excited they swooshed around the cave sending swirls of bubbles everywhere.

"Goodness," clicked Little Dolphin's mom. "It's like having a storm right here in the cave! Go and play. But don't go too far. You could get swept away — the currents are very strong. And don't go near the old wreck. It might not be safe in this weather."

"We won't, Mom," Little Dolphin grinned. "Let's go, Milo!"

Little Dolphin and Milo dashed through the choppy water toward Poppy's house. The storm was getting nearer. Out to sea, the sky was lit with bright jagged forks of

light and they could hear distant
rumbles out in the bay.

Poppy the spinner
dolphin was spinning
madly in circles in
the white-flecked
waves. "Hello,
you two," she
clicked. "Isn't
this great?"

"Do you
want to come and play with us?"
Little Dolphin asked.

"Yes, please!" chirped Poppy,
spinning even faster. "Let's play
shipwrecks. I'll be a whirlpool."

"I'm the ship, then!" exclaimed

Milo. He flapped his flippers and made loud creaking noises. "I'm sinking!"

"Here comes a tidal wave!" Little Dolphin whistled. He reared up on his tail, blew a huge *whoosh* through his blowhole and flopped on top of his friend. He and Milo sank down through the churning water onto the seabed. Poppy whizzed around them, whistling with delight.

"We've sunk him!" Little Dolphin squeaked as they collapsed in the sand.

There was a strange rustling. The three friends looked to see

what it was. Then, all of a
sudden, a grumpy face poked
out from a dark cave beside
them.

It was the old conger eel,
Cornelius—and he looked
furious!

CHAPTER TWO

"How dare you make all that noise!" Cornelius growled. "It's hard enough trying to have a nap in this storm, without silly little whippersnappers like you fooling around!"

"We...we...we're very sorry, Mr. Cornelius, sir," Little Dolphin apologized. They were outside Cornelius's cave, but nobody played near there on purpose. The stormy water must have swept them along the reef.

"Little Dolphin was pretending to be a tidal wave," explained Milo. "And I was a ship—so I had to sink."

"We were only playing," clicked Poppy nervously.

"Playing!" grunted the old eel. "You'd be better off shrimp-watching or shell-collecting—or something else that's quiet. Now go away and stop disturbing me."

The three friends didn't need to be told twice. They sped off as fast as they could.

"Cornelius is always so grumpy!" Little Dolphin declared, as they came to a stop on the other side of the reef. "We'd better do as he says, and keep away."

"Well, I'm not going shell-collecting," Poppy said firmly.

"Or shrimp-watching," squeaked Milo. "Let's play hide-and-seek instead!"

"Good idea," Little Dolphin chirped. "I'll count first." He closed his eyes and started to count while Milo and Poppy swooshed away to hide.

"...Ninety-eight, ninety-nine, one hundred...ready or not, here I come!" Little Dolphin called at last. He opened his eyes and had a quick look around. The sea was getting rougher, and the sand was being churned up in the strong currents. Not a dolphin in sight.

He knew where Poppy would be hiding. She had a favorite place—in the thick weeds, by the starfish caves. He went straight toward the two waving clumps of

rubbery seaweed, and poked his
nose into the first one he came to.

There was Poppy among
the leaves.

"How did you find me
so quickly?" she squeaked in
amazement.

"You always hide here!" Little Dolphin grinned.

"No, I don't!" clicked Poppy indignantly. "Sometimes I hide in the other bush."

"Well, I'm glad I found you," Little Dolphin said. "You can help me look for Milo now."

Little Dolphin and Poppy peered into the starfish caves. There was no one there.

"Let's try the other side of the reef," Little Dolphin suggested.

They set off, swimming over a bed of sleeping oysters, then under an arch of barnacle-covered rock. Eventually, they

came to the old wrecked ship that
lay on the seabed.

Poppy started to swim past,
but Little Dolphin stopped. The
wreck was a very good place to
hide, and he knew Milo loved
playing in it.

The old ship looked very
different in the storm. It was dark
down among the rotten wood.

Little Dolphin could see seaweed on its deck, waving in the stormy currents, like the tentacles of a giant octopus. He didn't like the idea of searching in there. It was much too scary. And anyway, his mom had told him and Milo it would be dangerous to play there during the storm.

Little Dolphin turned to swim on. But all of a sudden he heard a faint squeak from the wreck.

"Help!"

It was Milo!

Little Dolphin called Poppy back. "Milo's in the wreck!" he clicked anxiously. "And my mom said we shouldn't play in there today. He's so forgetful! We'd better get him out—and quickly!"

Little Dolphin and Poppy dived down through the broken wooden deck and peered into the dark, murky water. They couldn't see their friend anywhere.

"Where are you, Milo?" Little Dolphin called.

"Behind the treasure chest!" came Milo's voice. "Hurry! I'm stuck."

Little Dolphin swam toward

the big wooden chest with rusty metal hinges. Lying across the chest was a huge piece of timber. Suddenly, Little Dolphin saw Milo's nose poke out from behind it. It looked very funny.

"You fooled me, Milo," Little Dolphin grinned. "For a moment, I thought you really were stuck!"

But Milo's eyes were round and wide with fear. "This isn't a joke," he squeaked. "I *am* stuck!"

CHAPTER THREE

Poor Milo! Little Dolphin was very worried!

"Behind the treasure chest seemed like such a great hiding place," clicked Milo. "I was just squeezing in when suddenly this huge plank of wood fell down in front of me."

Little Dolphin felt the currents of water racing though the holes in the wreck and making the sand swirl. His mom was right. The old ship would be dangerous in a storm. The timbers were shifting and creaking all around them.

"What's going to happen when the storm gets here?" squealed Milo in alarm. "It'll all fall down on me!"

"Don't worry, Milo," Little Dolphin said, trying to sound brave. "We'll get you out of there before you can say slithering sea snakes! Let's move this plank, Poppy."

Little Dolphin put his flipper

over one end of the plank and
Poppy swam to the other. They
tried to heave it away from the
chest, but it just wouldn't budge.
They hooked their tails around the
wood and pulled with all their
might.

Still nothing happened. The
timber was too heavy for them.

"It didn't move as much as a shrimp's whisker!" groaned Poppy. "What are we going to do?"

Little Dolphin could see Milo's frightened eyes peering out from behind the chest. He had to find a way to free his friend. "We have to get help!" he whistled. "Come on, Poppy."

"Don't leave me alone!" squeaked Milo.

"I'll stay here with Milo," said Poppy bravely. She nuzzled Milo with her nose. "I'll keep you cheerful till Little Dolphin comes back."

"But how?" asked Milo miserably.

"Well, I know a new dance!" Poppy chirped brightly. "It's called the flip and spin. I'll show you."

"Better not!" clicked Little Dolphin hastily. "That might bring the wreck down on all of us!"

He thought quickly. "Do you remember the song we sang every day in Mrs. Haddock's play-group?" he asked.

"You mean, 'What Shall We Do with the Shrunken Sardine?'"

asked Milo, forgetting to be scared for the moment. "That was my favorite!"

"Great!" grinned Poppy. "We'll sing it while Little Dolphin goes for help."

"OK," agreed Milo. "Don't forget the verse about the dizzy old dogfish."

"We'll sing all twenty-three verses," Poppy promised him.

"And I'll be back before you've finished!" Little Dolphin chirped. Then he shot out of the wreck.

CHAPTER FOUR

The stormy water was even
rougher now, and the old ship
was groaning and swaying. There
was no time to lose! But where
could Little Dolphin turn for help?
He swam off fast across the bay,
but no one was in sight. Then he
realized that he was passing a
cave where he knew someone
was at home.

Cornelius! He felt a sudden
shiver run from his nose to his tail.
Oh, dear, he didn't want to disturb
the grumpy conger eel again. But
he had no choice! He stopped at
the entrance. He didn't dare go
any farther. It was dark and
gloomy, and he could hear a
terrible rumbling noise coming
from inside.

Cornelius must be waiting to pounce on anyone who came near!

Then Little Dolphin thought of poor Milo trapped in the creaking wreck, and he knew he had to be brave. He edged in slowly.

The rumbling noise echoed all around. Little Dolphin anxiously looked up and down. The sound was coming from the deepest, darkest corner. Little Dolphin swam closer, feeling very scared.

Now, at last, he could see Cornelius. The old conger eel

wasn't waiting for him after all.
He was snoring!

Little Dolphin could feel his
heart pounding. He would have
to wake up Cornelius. He gave
the old eel a gentle nudge. But
Cornelius just rolled over in his
sleep. Little Dolphin tapped him
with his flipper. Cornelius gave
a snort but he still didn't wake.
"Mr. Cornelius!" Little Dolphin
whistled loudly. "Please wake up!"

Cornelius's beady eyes
popped open and he sprang up.
"What's going on?" he growled.
"Who's there?"

Little Dolphin froze with fright

as the conger eel stared at him.
"I'm sorry, Mr. Cornelius, but—"

Cornelius whipped his tail
angrily. "Sorry?" he bellowed.
"Waking me up twice in one day!
You'll be sorry, when I tell your
mother!"

"But I need your help," Little
Dolphin insisted.

"Help?" Cornelius frowned,
swishing his tail angrily. "Is this
a joke? I've told you to leave me
alone. I don't want to see you
anywhere near this cave again!
Be off with you!"

Little Dolphin was trembling
all over, but he had to make

Cornelius understand. This was an emergency. "Milo's in trouble!" he squeaked. "He's stuck in the wreck! And Poppy's there with him! And they're singing songs to stay cheerful! And the storm's getting closer! And the wreck's going to squash him — and we're all so scared! Please help!"

Cornelius looked hard at him.

Oh dear, thought Little Dolphin, *he thinks I've made it all up!*

And then, slowly, the expression

on Cornelius's face changed. "Why didn't you say so right away?" he said, looking worried, too. "Of course I'll come with you."

"Do you know where the old wreck is, Mr. Cornelius?" Little Dolphin asked timidly as they swam along through the stormy waters.

"Of course," said Cornelius. "I used to play there all the time when I was a young eel! Things were different then, you know. We young eels never went around waking up our elders."

"We really didn't mean any harm," Little Dolphin said.

Cornelius grunted. "Maybe not," he said gruffly.

They swam up to the old wreck. Little Dolphin could see bits of wood breaking off its sides and swirl-ing away in the rough seas. He could hear his friends still singing. *"Put him in a barrel and roll him over..."*

As soon as Poppy and Milo saw the old conger eel, they gulped and stopped.

"It's all right," Little Dolphin said quickly. "Mr. Cornelius has come to help."

"Now then, young Milo," said Cornelius kindly. "You've gotten yourself into a mess, haven't you?"

Milo nodded glumly.

"We tried to move the wood," said Poppy, "but it was too heavy."

Cornelius swam up and down the length of the plank, prodding it with his nose. "It's a very solid piece of timber," he agreed. Then he turned and began to swim away.

Little Dolphin had thought Cornelius was going to help get Milo out. But instead he was leaving them! "Where are you going?" he clicked anxiously.

Cornelius stopped at the gap in the deck. "We can't shift that wood on our own," he said solemnly. "I'm going to fetch the Lobster Brigade!"

CHAPTER FIVE

"When's Cornelius coming back?"
squeaked Milo, as the three
friends waited for help to arrive.
"He's been gone for ages!"

The wreck swayed
dangerously in the churning
water. The storm was almost
overhead now and nobody felt
like singing anymore.

"The Lobster Brigade station's

not far away," Little Dolphin said. "He'll be back with Captain Capes and his crew as soon as he can."

All of a sudden they heard a loud blaring from a conch shell.

"It's their siren!" Poppy whistled with relief.

Cornelius appeared through the gap in the deck above. "The brigade's right behind me," he announced as he swam down to join them.

"At last!" exclaimed Milo. "I can feel the roof pressing down on me!"

A large, important-looking

lobster climbed down through the
hole and strutted toward them.
He was wearing a yellow hat
with a badge showing the words
LOBSTER BRIGADE and a pair of
crossed pincers on the back.

Two smiling lantern fish
darted alongside him, lighting up
the gloomy space under the deck
with their glow. "On the double,

men!" he shouted over his shoulder. "Hup, two, three, four! Hup, two, three, four!"

One by one, the Lobster Brigade appeared through the hole and dropped to the sand. Quickly, they formed two straight lines and marched along, shells gleaming. They each wore the Lobster Brigade hat, and the last two pulled a clamshell cart.

"HALT!" bellowed their leader. The brigade stopped in front of Little Dolphin and Poppy, and clicked their pincers in salute.

Little Dolphin slumped to the sand with relief. If anyone could rescue Milo, it was the Lobster Brigade. Their leader stepped forward and removed his helmet.

"Captain Capes at your service!" he announced. "Now, what have we got here?" He inspected Milo's prison and scratched his head. "Sergeant Gripper," he ordered, slapping his helmet back on, "prepare the brigade for dolphin removal!"

A crusty old lobster shuffled over to the cart. He handed ropes and hooks to the smallest member of the brigade, who disappeared under the huge pile.

"What are they going to do?"

squeaked Milo anxiously. "Will it hurt?"

"Certainly not," exclaimed

Captain Capes. "Private Pinch, tell the young dolphin our motto."

"Sorry, sir," came a voice from under the pile of equipment. "Don't know, sir!"

"It's his first day, Captain,"

explained Sergeant Gripper. "I
haven't taught him the motto yet."

"Let's hear our motto,
Brigade!" ordered Captain
Capes.

The Lobster Brigade stood
at attention. "You're safe in our
claws!" they chanted.

At that moment, there was a
loud rumble overhead.

Poppy shrieked and began to
spin around wildly.

"Stop that at once, Miss,"
ordered the captain. "Get to
work, everyone! There's no time
to lose!"

Poppy spun to
a halt. "Sorry," she
clicked.

"Lights over here!"
called Sergeant Gripper,
clicking his pincers.
The lantern fish darted over
and shone their lights at the timber
that was blocking Milo's way out.

Every lobster took a hook and
a rope. They screwed the hooks
into the timber and knotted the
ropes to them.

"Brigade, take
your positions!"
ordered Captain
Capes.

"Sergeant Gripper, untangle Private Pinch!"

The new recruit was hopping around, trying to untie himself from his rope. As soon as Sergeant Gripper got him free, the lobsters took their ropes firmly in their claws. The storm currents were racing around now, and they could hear thunder crashing overhead. It didn't look as if the wreck would hold out for much longer.

"Take the strain," ordered the captain, "and HEAVE!"

The ropes tightened as the Lobster Brigade pulled as hard as they could.

Nothing happened.

They dug their claws into the sand and pulled again. The heavy timber gave a small shudder and, at last, began to move away from the chest.

Milo poked his nose through the gap. He got one flipper free, then the other. But suddenly he stopped. "My fin's stuck!" he squeaked as he struggled.

"Brigade, heave again!"
shouted Captain Capes urgently.
The lobsters gave one last
heave. Milo wriggled and
twisted—and burst out of his
prison! Behind him the roof gave
way and collapsed in a pile of
broken wood.

Little Dolphin and the Lobster
Brigade gave a huge gasp—

and then a cheer! And Poppy,
remembering not to spin this
time, whistled loudly.

"Are you all right, Milo?"
asked Cornelius. "No cuts or
bruises?"

"I'm fine!" chirped Milo.
"Thank you, everybody. I
never would have gotten out
without your help!"

"All in a day's work!" said Captain Capes, with a salute. "And now my team must make the wreck safe. Ready, lobsters! Private Pinch, where are you?"

There was an odd grunting noise behind them. They turned to see the newest member of the Lobster Brigade, bright pink in the face and still tugging on his rope. "You're safe in our claws. You're safe in our claws!" he was muttering.

The three friends swam away from the wreck with Cornelius following.

"Thank you for getting the Lobster Brigade, Mr. Cornelius," said Milo, as they stopped at Cornelius's cave.

"Little Dolphin's mom said we shouldn't go near the wreck, but I forgot! I'm such a scatterbrain! I don't know what I'd have done without you."

"Don't mention it," Cornelius grunted, looking embarrassed.

The storm was raging right overhead now and the strong underwater currents were swirling around.

"The waves will be great!" squealed Poppy. "Last one to the surface is a silly sardine!"

Milo and Poppy raced away. Little Dolphin grinned. Milo had already forgotten his ordeal. He started to follow them, but then stopped. He couldn't leave Cornelius on his own, when they were going to have such fun.

"Would you like to come and play with us, Mr. Cornelius?" he asked shyly.

The old eel looked at him for a moment. Then something very strange happened. Cornelius smiled!

"I do believe I would enjoy that," he exclaimed. "Now don't forget what Poppy said— last one to the surface is a silly sardine!"

And Little Dolphin and Cornelius raced up to join the others and bounce around in the waves.